W9-DIE-530

Why Won't Winter Go?

Why Won't Winter Go?

by Lissa McLaughlin

Lothrop, Lee & Shepard Books   New York

Library of Congress Cataloging in Publication Data
McLaughlin, Lissa, (date)
    Why won't winter go?
    Summary: Bored with winter, Andy angrily protests the lingering
season until he finds a skunk cabbage, an early sign of spring.
    [1. Winter-Fiction. 2. Spring-Fiction] I. Title.
PZ7.M478698Wh 1983   [E]   83-723
ISBN 0-688-02380-0
ISBN 0-688-02381-9 (lib. bdg.)

FOR MEG

Andy was bored with Winter.
His nose was always cold.
His boots were always wet.
He was tired of buttoning
so many buttons.
"Will Winter last forever?"
he asked his sister Meg.
"I think it's spent enough time
here already."
"Give Winter a chance to go,"
said Meg.
"Don't you know the plants need
this little chance to rest?"

But Andy was mad.
He stood at the window, yelling,
"Winter, get out of here!"
"Andy, you're making it worse,"
Meg screamed.
She could hardly wait for
Spring herself.

The next morning snow was falling again.
Everyone knew Andy was coming
downstairs, from the angry noises
he was making.
"Andy, did you see the frost feathers?"
his mother asked.
"Of course I did," Andy said gloomily.
"How about going for a ride?"
Andy's father suggested.
"I have to buy some more sand
to sprinkle on the sidewalk."
"Phooey," said Andy.
"Why doesn't the snow just dry up?"

Andy spent all morning playing
explorer in the desert.
He wore a special hat
so the heat would not make him faint.
His camel helped him
carry things around.
"Andy!" called his mother,
"I'm making some nice hot soup
for lunch. Do you want some?"
"Oh, no, not more of that hot stuff!"
groaned Andy.
"I wish it were Spring
and we could eat ice cream!"

He made a sandwich
and put it in the refrigerator.
"Andy, what are you doing?"
asked Meg after a while.
"Eating my nice cold lunch," said Andy.

"Andy, let's go outside," said Meg.

"Put on your coat."

"What's out there?" asked Andy.

"You'll see," his sister said mysteriously.

They went out into the snow.

Soon Andy got tired of the crunching noise
his steps made in the snow.

"Aren't you tired of blowing your nose?" he asked Meg.
"I'm just sad my poor nose has to be red
   all the time," she said, giving it a pat.

But Andy wasn't listening.
"Look!" he yelled. "Our old clubhouse!"
"Is this the secret, Meg?"

They snuggled inside the clubhouse.
"Andy, imagine it's Spring already
and we can smell the flowers,"
said Meg.
"Can you smell them?"
"I think so," said Andy.
He shut his eyes.
He was trying hard to smell Spring.

Suddenly Meg darted out of the clubhouse.
"Where are you going?" Andy called.
"Let's play hide and seek!" yelled Meg.
"Andy, you're It!"

Andy ran deep into the woods.
"I see you!" he said.
"I see your hat!"

Then Andy saw something else.
"Look, Meg," he said. "I think
I see a plant!"

"Oh, Andy, I can't believe it!"
said Meg.
"You did find a plant.
And it's skunk cabbage,
a little plant that means
Spring is already on its way!"
Andy felt proud.
"Why is it called skunk cabbage?"
he asked.
"Because it's a little stinky,"
Meg smiled.
"Just like you!"

Andy and Meg looked for more
skunk cabbage in the woods.
They covered it with snow
after they looked at it,

so the skunk cabbage wouldn't
try to come up too early.
Andy could tell his sister liked
the little plants.

When they got home, he let Meg
wear his explorers' helmet.
He made hot cocoa for both of them.
Meg was still smiling
about the skunk cabbage outside.
"Andy," she said, "doesn't cocoa taste good
when it's cold?"
"Yes," Andy said, looking out the window.
"Cocoa tastes wonderful,
especially when it's almost Spring!"